Matthew Richey

A Sermon occasioned by the Death of the Rev. William Croscombe

SALZWASSER VERLAG

Matthew Richey

A Sermon occasioned by the Death of the Rev. William Croscombe

Reprint of the original, first published in 1859.

1st Edition 2022 | ISBN: 978-3-37512-172-3

Verlag (Publisher): Salzwasser Verlag GmbH, Zeilweg 44, 60439 Frankfurt, Deutschland
Vertretungsberechtigt (Authorized to represent): E. Roepke, Zeilweg 44, 60439 Frankfurt, Deutschland
Druck (Print): Books on Demand GmbH, In de Tarpen 42, 22848 Norderstedt, Deutschland

A

SERMON

OCCASIONED BY THE DEATH OF

THE REV. WILLIAM CROSCOMBE,

Preached in Windsor, 30th October, and in Halifax,
6th November, 1859.

BY THE

REV. MATTHEW RICHEY, D. D.

———

Halifax, N. S:
PRINTED AT THE WESLEYAN CONFERENCE STEAM PRESS.
1859.

SERMON.

HEBREWS, Chap. vi, Ver. 11, 12.

'Επιθυμουμεν δε εκαςον υμων την αυτην ενδεικνυςθαι σπουδην προς την πληροφοριαν της ελπιδος αχρι τελους· 'ινα μη νωθροι γενηςθε, μιμηται δε των δια πιςτεως και μακροθυμιας κληρονομουντων τας επαγγελιας.

"And we desire that every one of you do shew the same diligence to the full assurance of hope unto the end: that ye be not slothful, but followers of them who through faith and patience inherit the promises."

AMONG the dying utterances of a distinguished physician and philosopher,* enregistered by his biographer, there is one that strikes us as peculiarly memorable and monitory: "I have taken," he said, "I have taken what unfortunately the generality of Christians too much take,—I have taken the middle walk of Christianity: I have endeavored to live up to its duties and doctrines; but I have lived below its privileges." Who can fail to recognize in those impresssive words, a description—too accurate, alas! of the average living Christianity of even the brightest eras in the history of the Church? There is reason to apprehend that they reflect with humiliating precision, the sentiments and feelings with which by far the greater proportion of Christians enter the vale of death. From the auspicious dawn of the Divine life in the soul, we should augur better things. With the first impulses and aspirations of the love of Christ, the *first works* of those in whose hearts it is shed abroad, are usually in happy accord. They feel that they can never do enough to testify the gratitude of their exulting hearts to Him who has delivered them from the coming wrath. Their spirit and conversation are redolent of the celestial unction they have recently

---

* Dr. Gregory's Memoirs of Dr. Mason Good.'

received. Nothing, in their estimation, is worth living for, but to glorify God and win heavenly crowns. Would that the high and holy anticipations, created by such incipient effects of the power of godliness, were always realized by the issue! But, that the instances in which that is the case are comparatively few, is a fact not less manifest than it is mournful. Of those who become heirs of salvation, through faith in our Lord Jesus Christ, the proportion is lamentably small who avail themselves of the immense resources placed at their disposal by the gracious economy under which we live, to perfect holiness in the fear of God. Instead of rising to inhale the invigorating atmosphere and enjoy the heavenly prospects, that animate disciples who travel on the high-way of holiness, most of those who put on the Lord Jesus, take the middle walk of Christianity,—perhaps a lower position. They linger out an almost joyless and unprofitable existence in the vestibule of the Christian temple, though invited and urged by a thousand voices to enter into the Holiest, where the true Shekinah—the glory of God in the face of Jesus Christ—unveils its transforming lustres to the pure in heart.

The Apostles had occasion to bewail many such cases among Hebrew, as well as Heathen converts to the faith of Christ. To that class obviously belonged the persons to whom St. Paul addressed the scorching expostulations with which the preceding chapter closes, and the animated exhortations and awful warnings contained in this. Counsels so salutary, my brethren, can never be unseasonable; nor can the motives by which they are enforced ever lose their power. If it was the duty of the first Christians, it can be no less obligatory upon us, to leave the principles of the doctrine of Christ, and go on to perfection. If by neglecting a course so imperative, *they* were in danger of falling away so utterly as to become judicially abandoned to the hopelessness of irreclaimable impenitence and the desolation of an undone eternity; *we*, though placed in different circumstances, are by no means unconditionally exempted from liability to woe equally overwhelming. Our safety depends upon our fidelity to the grace of God: our reception of the

Divine benediction, on our bringing forth the fruits of righteousness, of which the spiritual culture bestowed upon us ought of right to be productive: in a word, our eternal salvation depends on our being *followers of them who, through faith and patience inherit the promises.*

The Scriptures present a wide range of topics relevant to occasions like the present. In giving the preference to the subject announced in the text, as suggestive of reflections especially appropriate to the event which it is our object to improve, I have in following the prompting of my best judgment, obeyed at the same time, the spontaneous impulse of my heart. All who were acquainted with the justly venerated Minister of Christ, whom God has been pleased, after a long and honorable career, to call to his eternal reward, will, I am quite sure, unhesitatingly acquiesce in the propriety of the selection. His life was a model of holy diligence in the service of his Divine Master;—his end was peace;—and, that his sainted spirit is now added to the ever-expanding cloud of witnesses by whom we are encircled, no one, it is apprehended, entertains a doubt.

How then can I turn the present opportunity to better account than by affectionately urging you who revere the memory, to imitate the example, of our departed Brother ?

This I shall endeavour to do by developing in order, the principle recognized; the counsel administered; and the motive suggested, by the Apostle in the text.

I. *We are under solemn obligations to emulate the virtues of departed believers, who have bequeathed to us an example of earnest and persevering fidelity in the service of God.*

This is the principle here assumed : and however it may be disposed of in practice, it can not fail, in theory at least, to command universal recognition.

It is not possible fully to estimate the value of an example of holy living, sustained in undeviating consistency through life's temptations and changefulness, for a long series of years. Such an impersonation of the power of godliness is the divinest spectacle seen on earth; imaging in no obscure manner to mortal eyes, those forms of redeemed humanity—the spirits of just men made perfect—that move in a loftier sphere. It is a moral demonstration of the saving efficiency as well as Divine origin of the Gospel—the best practical exponent at once of its creed and of its code—and infinitely more effective than all the wisdom and eloquence of words, in winning human hearts to the obedience of faith. Of the treatises on the Evidences of Revelation that enrich our literature, the feeblest possesses sufficient force to repress the malignant triumph of Infidelity, and evince the immovable permanence of the foundations on which the righteous repose. Yet, after all, the various phases and follies, the supercilious sneers and seductive sophisms of a speculative or a licentious scepticism, receive their most withering rebuke and refutation from the sanctity in life and the serenity in death, of those who, whether in an humble or elevated position, adorn the doctrine of God their Saviour in all things. Elaborate defences of religion few will take the pains to read; and many, if they did read, want the ability to appreciate them: but those "are epistles known and read of all men; forasmuch as they are manifestly declared to be the epistles of Christ, written not with ink, but with the Spirit of the living God." On this noiseless but most potent species of agency does Christianity place its main dependence, for the diffusion of its influence and the establishment of its empire over the souls of men.

It is in this aspect that the relations Christians sustain to the unconverted, and the grave responsibilities which those relations involve, are most impressively manifested. "Ye," says the Saviour, "Ye are the light of the world. A city that is set on a hill can not be hid. Neither do men light a candle and put it under a bushel, but on a candlestick, and it giveth light unto all that are in the house. Let your light so shine before men, that they may see your good works, and glorify your Father which is in heaven." St. Paul, in like manner, urges believers to act in a way worthy of their high adoption, by reminding them that they are the luminaries of this dark world; which must forever remain dark, unless they reflect upon it the light wherewith the Sun of Righteousness irradiates them.

But it must not be forgotten that the deep responsibilities associated with this view of Christian consistency, do not all lie on one side. If it is the imperative duty of all who name the name of Christ, by the assiduous cultivation and unostentatious display of the beauties of holiness, to sustain the honors of their Saviour and hold forth the word of life; a correlative responsibility as certainly devolves upon those whose privilege it is to witness such exemplifications of holy rectitude and heavenly mindedness, to walk by the same rule and mind the same thing. The obligation is mutual. The marvellous perspicacity that some persons evince, in detecting the faults and infirmities of professors of godliness, painfully contrasts with their apparent blindness to the conspicuous excellences of those against whom they can find no occasion, unless they find it against them concerning the law of their God. This disposition is the sworn antagonist of all benignant and softening influences from on high. It hardens the heart, and if long indulged, sears the conscience as with a hot iron. Moreover, it represses a potent moral instinct which the inspiration of the Almighty has breathed into the heart of redeemed humanity; and of which earthly ambition is but the perversion. When we read in classic story of Themistocles spending sleepless nights meditating on the trophies of Miltiades, we mark the operation of a principle, which, seized and sanctified by grace, would take the character of holy emulation, and covet earnestly the highest honors of those who, in their day, were valiant for the truth and did exploits.

However powerfully the example of holy men of God may make itself felt during life, it acquires new influences, and a more solemn authority over the conscience, from their death. Their Christian virtues, partially dimmed by the medium through which we contemplated them when they had their dwelling among us, have brightened in the purer atmosphere that now surrounds them, into a halo of unshaded refulgence: and the precious memories of their work of faith, and labor of love, and patience of hope, come at times rushing to the heart, like voices issuing from amidst the solemn grandeurs of eternity. The very fact, that, in their case, the great problem of probationary existence has received its solution—that they have reached the goal amidst the gratulations of the rejoicing myriads with whom they are henceforth to be associated forever—that God, even their own God, has stamped their approved character with the signet of eternity;—that fact alone might well stir our souls to their central depths, and brace us for the battle of life. If they conquered—so may we. If they are inaugurated priests and kings of immortality, the same sacred and imperial dignities await us, if we only imbibe their spirit and emulate their example.

And, if we neglect to do so, tell me, my brethren, what shall we be able to allege before the judgment seat of Christ;—what can we even now plead at the tribunal of our own conscience, in extenuation of the turpitude of our guilty supineness?

Do you allege your constitutional depravity, or the deceitfulness and domination of some particular sin, fortified in the ascendency it has acquired over you by the power of habit, or the influence of evil associations, from which, if you have the desire, you want the resolution to break away?

Consider calmly the true nature of such an apology for continuing in sin, and say candidly, whether instead of alleviating it does not really aggravate your guilt. O! beware of adding to your other delinquencies the sin of thus virtually imputing the blame of your conduct to that God who can not be tempted with evil; neither tempteth He any man. And, let me ask, have you lost sight of the fact that among the redeemed millions who make heaven vocal with hallelujahs to God and the Lamb, there is not one who was not by nature just as depraved as yourself?—not one who had not some strong impulsive proclivity to evil which, yielded to, would have lost him heaven, and assigned him his portion with hypocrites and unbelievers? Those robes, stainless as the bosom of a seraph, in which the saints in light are arrayed, were not always thus pure; nor would they ever have become so had they not washed and made them white in the blood of the Lamb. Those palms in their hands,—those crowns, corruscant with the jewelry of heaven, that sparkle on their heads, tell most impressively of many a fiery conflict—of many a glorious victory achieved over the powers of darkness;—tell of the crucifixion of the flesh with its affections and lusts; aye, and of the cutting off a right hand and plucking out a right eye, rather than forfeit the bliss they now enjoy. Obtain and exercise like precious faith,—form the same high resolves,—practice the same self-denial; and the loftiest barriers that obstruct your passage to the skies will crumble into dust beneath your feet.

Looking at your own weakness,—conscious not only of your alienation from God, but of your native enmity against Him; and feeling that when you would do good, evil is present with you; are you tempted to regard the inspiring hope of success, by which we seek to encourage and animate your efforts to follow departed saints as they followed Christ, as nothing better than a brilliant illusion? Look also, we beseech you, at the divine resources of grace provided for you by the transcendent sacrifice of the Cross, and which the Holy Ghost is ever ready to make available to the earnest seekers of salvation. Those resources, which the people of God have in every age found abundantly adequate to meet all their exigencies, still exist in undiminished amplitude, and are just as easy of access and appropriation to you as they were to them. An important element, indeed, in their present blesssedness, is a vivid and ineffaceable remembrance of the dangers to which they were ofttimes exposed and the delivering grace, never withheld in time of need,—of their soul-struggles, when, being in an agony they prayed the more earnestly, but never prayed in vain,—of their conscious helplessness, and the might of the indwelling Spirit, in virtue of which "out of weakness they were made strong, waxed valiant in fight, and turned to flight the armies of the aliens." Without the peace-speaking blood of Jesus they could never have tasted the joy of pardon;—without the gift of the Spirit they never could have conquered sin or experienced deliverance from its pollution; nor without the exceeding great and precious promises of the better covenant, could they have claimed in faith that participation of the Divine nature which constituted their meetness for the celestial inheritance. But *with* these resources they could, and did, cast their souls on the atonement, and joy in God through our Lord Jesus Christ, by whom they received it; they could and did say with exultant confidence, "Who shall separate us from the love of Christ? * * * I am persuaded, that neither death, nor life, nor angels, nor principalities, nor powers, nor things present, nor things to come, nor height, nor depth, nor any other creature, shall be able to separate us from the love of God which is in Christ Jesus our Lord."

Now, has the blood of Jesus lost aught of its virtue? Are the energies of the Eternal Spirit exhausted or impaired? Is He straitened? or has it ceased to be his great function to glorify Christ? Which of the promises of the word of salvation has God revoked? The echo of these questions reverberates in every heart; they lodge a conviction in every conscience that if any man fail of the grace of God, or follow not those who through faith and patience inherit the promises, the fault is all his own.

Our illustrations and arguments on this branch of our subject are far from being exhausted. Enough, however, has, we trust, been said, not only to procure the intellectual acquiescence of all in the principle that underlies the admonition of the text; and to stir up the pure minds of the people of God by way of remembrance; but also to elicit from the hearts of some who have never set forth in the Christian race, the repentant enquiry, "*Lord! what wilt Thou have me to do?*"

To that solemn question an answer is found in the delineation here given by the Apostle of the character of those whom he holds up as patterns for our imitation,—a delineation very brief indeed, but lucid, discriminating, and comprehensive, notwithstanding.

II. Let me invite you, then, in the second place, *to contemplate that character, in those aspects to which especial prominence is here given for our learning.*

And those, you will readily perceive, embrace the essential elements of that holiness without which no man shall see the

Lord;—energetic zeal in doing and suffering the will of God, vitalized and supported by *faith* and *patience*—the very soul and spirit of the inner Christian life.

Not by high profession, but by holy practice; not by yielding to the seducing solicitations of inglorious sloth, but by girding up the loins of their minds, and awaiting as faithful and wise stewards, the advent of their Lord,—did those whom we are exhorted to follow, achieve that most enviable of all distinctions, —the distinction of exemplary devotedness to the service of God.

"Not every one that saith unto me, Lord, Lord, shall enter into the kingdom of heaven; but he that doeth the will of my Father which is in heaven." This is, by eminence, the divine criterion of genuine discipleship: and no subtle casuistry is required in its application. Every man's conscience is quite competent, with the aid of that single luminous enunciation of the Great Teacher, to determine his character in the sight of God; and, if permitted to speak out, it will not fail to do so.

The same test we are authorized to apply to others: "By their fruits ye shall know them." "Let no man deceive you: he that doeth righteousness is righteous even as he is righteous. He that committeth sin is of the devil; for the devil sinneth from the beginning. For this purpose the Son of God was manifested, that he might destroy the works of the devil. Whosoever is born of God doth not commit sin: for his sin remaineth in him and he cannot sin, because he is born of God." With such declarations ringing in our ears, we are the victims of voluntary deception, if we imagine that zeal for any system of ecclesiastical polity or denominational peculiarities of doctrine, however correct and scriptural may be the theories to which we give our adhesion, can save us. The truth itself may be, and often is, held in unrighteousness; but the tenacity with which it is *thus* held, so far from mitigating, will rather aggravate the wrath of God, which is revealed from heaven against all ungodliness and unrighteousness of men. "Circumcision is nothing; and uncircumcision is nothing, but the keeping of the commandments of God."

Christianity institutes an elevated standard of duty; but not more elevated than is demanded alike by an enlightened regard to the glory of God and our own happiness. It requires the undivided and continuous consecration of our energies, physical, mental and moral, to Him from whom all our talents are received in trust. It throws its authority and hallowing influence not merely over those offices and performances that are generally regarded as properly belonging to the sphere of religion; but likewise over the most ordinary occupations and enjoyments of life; so that whether we eat or drink, or whatsoever we do, we are bound to do all to the glory of God.

Repellent as the lustre of a code so pure cannot but be to those whose deeds are evil, its purity is, in point of fact, its strongest attraction to all whose hearts are right with God. To such His commandments are not grievous; nor is the blessedness connected with obedience to them altogether reversionary: the experience of the faithful attests that IN keeping of them there is great reward. Yes: there is the peace of God which passeth all understanding; there is, as the text expresses it, *the full assurance of hope*—an evidence of acceptance, and a delightful sense of communion with God, that not only authorise, but, by a species of moral necessity, generate and sustain a confiding and joyful anticipation of eternal felicity. This consoling and victorious hope it was, by virtue of which the believing Hebrews not only sustained with meekness the storms of persecution that poured their fury upon them on their embracing Christianity; but took *joyfully* the spoiling of their goods, knowing in themselves that they had in heaven a better and an enduring substance.

Nor has the excelling glory of the "Ministration of the Spirit" in this respect at all waned. It is as full-orbed at the present hour as it was when the Sun of Righteousness rose with healing in his wings. Was it a privilege, think you, peculiar to the first followers of the Redeemer to give utterance to their motives in the language of the beloved disciple—"Behold what manner of love the Father hath bestowed upon us, that we should be called the sons of God!"—or, in the contemplation of death, to say with Paul, "We know that if our earthly house of this tabernacle be dissolved, we have a building of God, an house not made with hands, eternal in the heavens?" Rest assured, my brethren, that such low views—too prevalent, it is to be regretted, amongst those who profess and call themselves Christians,—result from making, not the uncorrupted Gospel of Christ, but a deteriorated type of Christianity, at once the rule of their duty and the guage of their privileges. But, free and abounding as is the grace of God, He does not, let it be well observed, waste such precious immunities, as "the full assurance of hope," on the unfaithful, the negligent, and the formal. "He that hath this hope in him purifieth himself even as Christ is pure." His hope lives by the constant exercise of its hallowing power. Unless it satisfy that condition it must inevitably perish. Let moral relaxation impair its ardent, impulsive energy, and there must come over it a blight—a moral mildew, that, unless quickening grace preclude the disastrous issue, will soon despoil it of its bloom, and lay it, effete and withered, on the ground. The divine models on which the text fixes our attention, were characterised by the wakeful and stern resistance offered to the paralyzing influence of spiritual sloth, and by the self-denying cultivation of all the activities of practical godliness appropriate to the spheres in which they were severally placed by the providence of God. Thus it was, that they walked in the light as He is in the light, having fellowship with Him, and experiencing the joy of the Lord to be their strength: and thus it is, that, if we would make our calling and election sure, we must, like them, give all diligence to work out our own salvation, and to serve our generation according to the will of God. No longer then, shall we have to complain that the consolations of God are small with us: our path, on the contrary, will answer to the beautiful description of that of the just—it will shine more and more unto the perfect day.

To consummate the progressive lustre and loveliness of the Christian's course "a patient continuance in well-doing" is indispensable. Hence the intense solicitude expressed by the Apostle in the text, that his believing countrymen should, by the unwavering decision of holy purpose, and the unwearied energy of holy action, hold their first confidence steadfast to the end. And this salutary counsel, which the feelings that dictated it, prompted him rather affectionately to insinuate than authoritatively to enjoin, it behooves all who would share in the celestial inheritance equally to regard. The crown of life is reserved for those who are faithful unto death. St. Paul, whose history from the time of his conversion, was a translucent illustration of the precepts he inculcated, has bequeathed to the Church an illustrious example of persistent fidelity in the face of the most appalling opposition ever encountered by man; from the contemplation of which many a pious heart, tremulous with apprehension has learned to triumph over difficulties that before seemed insuperable,—"Not as though I had already attained," declares this devoted disciple and intrepid champion of the Cross,—"Not as though I had already attained, either were already perfect: but I follow after, if that I may apprehend that for which I also am apprehended of Christ Jesus. Brethren, I count not myself to have apprehended: but this one thing I do, forgetting those things which are behind, I press towards the goal, for the prize of the high calling of God in Christ Jesus." Who can wonder that a career prosecuted on such principles, and in such a spirit, should close so triumphantly;—that, in planting his foot upon the verge of the sepulchre—I would say—in ascending the altar of martyrdom as a willing sacrifice—the venerable Apostle should be heard to exclaim,—" I am now ready to be offered up, and the time of my departure is at hand. I have fought the good fight, I have finished the course, I have kept the faith. Henceforth there is laid up for me the crown of righteousness, which the Lord, the righteous judge, will give me in that day."

Energy and excellence of character of a nature so peculiar, clearly attest the Divine origin of the principles that constitute its source and support: they conduct us to the *inner life* of the believer;—that life which, in its essence, is hid with Christ in God, whilst its influence is manifested in the fruits of righteousness and true holiness.

Such a character, no maxims of ethical science, no labors of moral philosophy, no plastic power of education;—no nor earnest inculcation of the laws of the Decalogue itself, though written by the finger, and clothed with the majesty of the living God—ever did, or ever could form. It is a Divine creation. The Lord, the Spirit, by the operation of His mighty power, forms it out of the ruins of our apostacy, and breathes into it the breath of life.

We have seen the moral symmetry of its *form;* but our estimate will be very imperfect, unless it comprehend an inspection of the principles of its interior *life.* The most efficient of these, according to the analysis of the Apostle, are *faith* and *patience.*

The primal element of spiritual life is *faith:* not a theory, a speculation, a cherished dogma; but a vital, operative principle —a grace of the Holy Spirit—the inseparable concomitant, and precious instrument, of all the other virtues that adorn the character of those who are born from above. This faith is one of those " things of the Spirit of God," which the natural, that is to say the unconverted, unspiritual man, does not understand ; neither can he know them, for they are spiritually discerned. He may believe in the inspiration of the Scriptures, and be unexceptionably orthodox in his views of the system of theology deducible from them ; but, of the fact that *with the* HEART *man believeth unto righteousness,* he can have no experimental perception, until He who commanded the light to shine out of darkness, shine in his heart, to give the light of the knowledge of the glory of God, in the face of Jesus Christ. A merely logical or historical faith— a purely intellectual acquiescence in the teachings of the sacred Oracles—never yet embraced and appropriated the promises of God ; never purified a human heart ; never triumphed over the world's lusts ; never poured the light of eternity on the mind's eye, imparting the substance of things hoped for, the evidence of things not seen. No : these are the achievements of a diviner principle—of that faith, namely, which is of the operation of God, and which invariably works by love. By this principle the people of God have in every age been characterised. Whatever diversities may have existed among them, in this they have ever agreed : they were all *partakers of like precious faith.*

This was the secret, at once of their power with God and of the most beneficent influence they exercised over their fellow-men. In short: their work and labor of love,—their entire course of active and of submissive obedience to the will of Heaven, were but the practical evolution of that sacred and mighty principle. Here, then, our endeavors to imitate them must begin; and the surest test of our success, at every subsequent period, will be the sincerity and loving confidence wherewith we are enabled to aver, "I am crucified with Christ: nevertheless I live; yet not I, but Christ liveth in me: and the life that I now live in the flesh, I live by the faith of the Son of God, who loved me and gave himself for me."

Another characteristic of those whose example ought to excite our emulation, to which the Apostle gives especial prominence, is their *patience*—or, as the very significant word μακροθυμιας properly means, *longanimity*, or *enduring patience*. Patience, simply, is exemplified whenever any trial is sustained in a spirit of meekness, however brief the period of trial may be: but longanimity is patience indefinitely protracted—patience, the exercise of which is renewed with every trial; and whose power of **endurance** is neither broken down by the intensity, nor exhausted by the continuance, of the ordeals through which it is called to pass.

The unspeakable importance of this *enduring* and *waiting* patience to the Christian must be palpable to all. It is, in fact, the perpetual recurrence of occasions, of one sort or another, for the exercise of this grace, that constitutes life, emphatically, a *probation*. So essential is it, that without it no progress is made, no maturity attained, in the divine life. "Let patience have its perfect work," exhorts St. James, "that ye may be perfect and entire, wanting nothing:" words which obviously indicate, that every other element of spiritual life will be dwarfed or developed, paralyzed or perfected, just in proportion as we possess our souls in patience, amid the disappointments, conflicts and vexations, that are permitted, in equal wisdom and love, by our Father in heaven, for the trial of our faith.

By the frequent association of the terms "faith" and "patience" in the phraseology of the Scriptures, we are forcibly reminded of the vital connexion of the qualities they designate, in the experience and history of the true believer. Stoic philosophy,—according to which the universe of mind and matter, and the Deity himself, are abandoned to the blind influence of *fate*,—may, by extinguishing the finest susceptibilities of the heart, foster a cold, self-relying apathy: but that intelligent, tranquil, and holy submission to the will of God, denoted in the sublime ethics of Christianity by the term " patience," and which, instead of annihilating, purifies and invigorates the affections, can emanate only from unfeigned faith. Patience, on the other hand, reciprocates the advantages it derives from faith, by increasing its might, and preparing it for higher rewards, that it may be found unto praise, and honor, and glory, at the revelation of Jesus Christ.

As there is no attribute traceable in the character of departed believers more exemplary than their patience, so there is none, commonly, more attractively conspicuous. You see it in their meekness under provocation and injury: "Being reviled they bless; being persecuted they suffer it; being defamed they entreat:"—You see it in their deep, filial submission to the Father of spirits, not seldom under crushing afflictions and desolating bereavements:—You see it in the more than heroic firmness they have, in countless instances, displayed, when proscription, imprisonment, and death in its most terrific forms, were the test, of their fidelity:—You see it in the implicit repose on the faithfulness, wisdom, and goodness of their covenant God, when surrounded by mysteries of His providence, of which their reason could neither interpret the meaning, appreciate the justice, nor anticipate the end : and you see it in their untiring discharge of the duties of life and godliness, through a long cycle of probation, overshadowed often towards its close, and sometimes in its progress, with infirmities, temptations and pain. From the severer tests to which many who have preceded you in the kingdom and patience of Christ, have been subjected, you, my brethren, are likely to enjoy an exemption. Yet, ye too—and perhaps not less than they—"have need of patience, that after ye have done the will of God, ye may receive the promise." It would, indeed, be as unwise in you to desire, as it were vain to anticipate, immunity from trials in this probationary scene of being. They enter essentially into that disciplinary system, by which it is the benignant design of your heavenly Father to train you for a higher sphere of existence. Think it not strange, then, if He permit even *fiery* trials to assay —so to speak—the metal of your principles, in order to test their real quality, and separate the alloy of baser ingredients from the gold of true grace. It is *good*—not merely pleasing to God, but profitable to yourselves,—that you both hope and quietly wait for the salvation of God. While you look not at the things which are seen, but at the things which are not seen, you possess the animating assurance of Him who cannot lie, that your light affliction, which is but for a moment, worketh out for you a far more exceeding and eternal weight of glory. To give full effect to this consideration, St. Paul, in the passage before us, withdraws the veil that hides that glory from mortal view: and we behold the faithful who have passed away from earth, in the actual fruition of its unimaginable blesssedness. He unequivocally asserts

III. *That those who were characterized by holy diligence and patient faith, on earth, now inherit the promises in heaven.*

Let not the rude hand of destructive criticism presume to tear from our hearts a testimony so precious. From reverent scrutiny we have nothing to fear. One of the ripest scholars of the age, especially in the department of sacred philology and exegesis, thus elicits and vindicates the genuine meaning of the word St. Paul here employs:—"κληρονομουντων. The only true interpretation of this word is that of the ancient and most modern Commentators, who take it as an *Aorist*, and explain,— ' who have come into the enjoyment of the promised blessing of salvation,' understanding the κλη. as referring partly to the patriarchs, their pious progenitors, who lived by faith in the promises of salvation through the future Saviour; and partly to those Hebrew Christians, who, imitating the faith and patience of their ancestors, had fought the good fight of faith and endured to the end and ; being at length delivered from their toils, had entered into the joy of their Lord promised to all his faithful servants. The plural in *ἐπαγγ.* as Kuinoel observes,—'is used because the promises in question were extended to the Patriarchs generally, and were given at various times and seasons (see Gen. xii, 3 ; xxii. 16 and 18 ; xxvi. 3 ; xxviii, 13) all, however, centering in the promise of salvation through a Redeemer.'" *

Thus the *obvious* reference in these expressions to the joy and felicity of departed saints, is sustained by the soundest principles of interpretation. And thus understood, how richly suggestive are they of just and elevated views of the heavenly state! Our time will permit me to do little more than indicate those views; but I trust you will expand them by your own meditation. In the word, *inherit*, there is a latent allusion —eminently apposite as addressed to Hebrew Christians— to Canaan, the standing type to the Church of God, of that sabbatic rest, the enjoyment of which awaits all the spiritual seed of the father of the faithful, after the weary pilgrimage of life. And oh! how refreshing to look away from the waste and howling wilderness through which we are now passing to the land of perennial verdure and pure delight; to solace ourselves amidst the harassings of our circuitous sojourn, with the thrilling thought that, if faithful, we shall soon, very soon, come, not in the anticipations of hope, but in the realizations of actual possession, to Mount Zion, the city of the living God, the heavenly Jerusalem which is the mother, and destined inheritance of us all! O come, consummation most blessed!

> Jerusalem! my happy home!
> When shall I come to thee,
> When shall my sorrows have an end,
> Thy joys when shall I see ?

Another thought emanating from this pregnant expression, and corroborated by the congenial significance, in this connexion, of the associated word *promises*, is,—that heaven is not the

---

* Dr. Bloomfield's Greek Test., with English notes, in loc.

acquisition of human merit, but the munificent donative of Divine mercy; that our final as well as present salvation, is not of works but of grace;—that, while death is the *wages* of sin, eternal life is the *gift* of God, through Jesus Christ our Lord. And this evangelical view of the matter is further illustrated and confirmed by the fact, that, as the kingdom of heaven is, in regard to man, not an original possession, but an inheritance; so that inheritance devolves to no human being by virtue of natural relationship or legal transmission; but purely by the gratuitous *promise* of God, who is in Christ reconciling an alienated world to himself. The Pauline argument in the third chapter of the epistle to the Galatians, on the topic of justification, is equally applicable and cogent here : " For if the inheritance be of the law it is no more of promise : but God gave it to Abraham by promise. * * * The scripture hath included all under sin, that the promise by faith of Jesus Christ might be given to them that believe."

It is as "heirs of promise," then, and not as legal claimants, that believers are entitled to rejoice in hope of the glory of God ; and, therefore, just in proportion as the Holy Spirit enables them thus to rejoice, are their hearts in unison with the sublime ascription—Blessed be the God and Father of our Lord Jesus Christ, who, according to his abundant mercy, hath begotten us again to a lively hope, by the resurrection of Jesus Christ from the dead, to an inheritance incorruptible, and undefiled, and that fadeth not away.

The transcendent grandeur of the inheritance of the saints in light, it is reserved for that day fully to disclose, when Christ shall come to be glorified in his saints, and to be admired in all them that believe. Not till then—shall these bodies of our humiliation, restored from the dishonors of the grave, be assimilated to the glorious body, in which our Redeemer now sits on His mediatorial throne. Not till then—shall the evolutions and accomplishments of the great redeeming plan reach the grand crisis of their consummation, and the acclaim of final triumph thunder through the temple of God. But, while this is freely admitted, far from our hearts be the thought that the blessed hope of glory which animates the real Christian shall be deferred till that illustrious day. We have just been singing—

> The saints who die of Christ possest,
> Enter into *immediate* rest;
> For them no further test remains,
> Of purging fires, and torturing pains.

Some, however, who explode the Pagan and Papal doctrine of purgatory, imagine that the soul, on its separation from the body, lapses into a condition of torpor, in which it will remain, insensible to the weal or woe of its eternal destiny, and unconscious even of its own existence, till the period of the resurrection. To whatever source this notion may be traced, it certainly was not derived from either the earnest of the Spirit in the believing heart, or the testimony of the Spirit in the written word. Intimately allied to that materialistic philosophy, which, unfortunately for the theory, is as unfavorable to the *immortality* of the soul, as to its self-consciousness in the intermediate state between death and the resurrection, it is only less revolting than annihilation itself to the spiritually-minded. From the bewildering glare of science, falsely so called, turn we to Him who has abolished death, and brought life and immortality to light. Does he not demonstrate from the covenant relation which God sustains to the patriarchs that they are now living? " for He is not the God of the dead but of the living; for all live to him." (Luke xx: 38.) Does he not, in the instance of the rich man and Lazarus,—whether regarded as a real history or a parable,—unveil the spirit world, and discover to us the souls of the departed, imparadised or tormented, according to their character? Did he not declare to the malefactor on the cross—" To day shalt thou be with me in paradise?" What heart instinct with the love of Christ could ever have glowed with a desire to depart; who could ever have triumphed in the hour or in the expectation, of dissolution—if to be absent from the body were not, to the Christian, to be present with the Lord —if to be unclothed of this material vehicle were not to be clothed upon with our house which is from heaven, that mortality might be swallowed up of life? Blessed be God, who

given us everlasting consolation and good hope through grace—
we have proofs as assuring and abundant as faith can desire,
that they who have died in the Lord, instead of being in a
state of somnolent insensibility, are now with Christ, all animate with the joy ineffable and eternal, implied in their inheriting *the promises*. I must repress my inclination to expatiate on
the various elements that constitute their blessedness. More
impressive than any systematic exposition of this lofty theme,
are those apocalyptic descriptions by the prophet of Patmos, in
which we see heaven opened, and unnumbered multitudes of all
nations, and kindreds, and people and tongues, standing before
the throne, and before the Lamb, clothed with white robes, and
palms in their hands: and crying with a loud voice, saying,
Salvation to our God, which sitteth upon the throne, and unto
the Lamb. * * * * They shall hunger no more, neither thirst
any more, neither shall the sun light on them, nor any heat.
For the Lamb which is in the midst of the throne, shall feed
them, and shall lead them unto living fountains of waters; and
God shall wipe away all tears from their eyes." Contrasted
with the substantial lustre and beatitude of such a destiny,
earth's richest pleasures and most envied honors—the glitter of
affluence, and the gayeties of dissipation, appear—what they
really are—dust and shadows.

With those who are inheriting the promises we have the best
reasons for believing that the beloved and honoured servant of
Christ, over whose mortal frame, worn by the labors of almost
half a century, and wasted with sickness and suffering, the
grave has recently closed, is now numbered.

It is not my intention to attempt a minute appreciation, much
less, a labored eulogy of his character. Let me glorify God in
him, while I pay a short, yet affectionate, tribute to his memory.
It is a duty, permit me to say, which I perform with melancholy
satisfaction; and by the assignment of which to me, under the
circumstances, I feel myself especially honored.*

---

* The writer received the intelligence of Mr. Croscombe's death when on an
official visit to Newfoundland: and this discourse was in consequence not
preached till two months after his decease.

The spiritual history of a "man of God" properly dates from the time when, by the mysterious but mighty agency of the Holy Spirit, he is renewed after the image of Him that created him in righteousness and true holiness. This is that great and decisive change which marks the transition of the penitent seeker of salvation from death to life—his deliverance by the Father from the power of darkness, and translation into the kingdom of the Son of His love. In virtue of this blessed change his faculties acquire a new development; he enters into new relations to Him of whom the whole family in heaven and earth is named. Sin having no longer dominion over him, he is placed under the dynasty of holy principles, which, if he receive not the grace of God in vain, will reign through righteousness unto eternal life. What a momentous epoch! Well may its circumstances be ineffaceably impressed on the memory of the regenerate heart! Thus it was with our venerable Brother who has fallen asleep in Jesus. Referring—in a brief epitome of his religious experience, written a short time previous to his death—to the time and place of his spiritual birth, his words are: " Glory be to God! I can testify this to be a genuine work of grace, after a trial of upwards of fifty years!"

Mr. Croscombe's piety was of a peculiarly attractive type. It was pre-eminently fitted to extinguish in those who witnessed his joyous alacrity in the service of his Divine Master, the unjust suspicion, that religion is unfriendly to present happiness. The benignant radiance of his countenance, which almost invariably reflected the interior sunshine of the soul; and the elasticity with which his spirit—naturally sensitive though it was—threw off the pressure of trials and afflictions, and armed itself for new enterprises of duty, attested the resources of a life hid with Christ in God. The joy of the Lord was his strength; and in felicitous combination with a constitutional amiableness of disposition, it imparted to his example a more than ordinary degree of the *beauty* of holiness. The doubts and apprehensions that overshadowed his mental serenity at times during his last illness, cannot be regarded as affording a true index of his spiritual state, or as at all inconsistent with what I have expressed, since they obviously resulted from the depressive influence of physical paralysis and prostration on the intellectual and emotional powers, and were followed by established peace, and, in the closing scene, a holy triumph over the last enemy.

In close and congenial alliance with the cheerful character of his piety; and forming, in fact, an efficient and pervasive element in its composition; there was observable in our departed friend, such an habitual recognition of the goodness of God, that he exemplified as perfectly as any one whom I have known, the apostolic precept, *In every thing give thanks*. All who had an intimate acquaintance with his spirit and communications, must retain a vivid remembrance of the fervor and frequency with which he was wont to give utterance to such devout ejaculations as, "Praise the Lord!" "Blessed be His holy name!" The tender mercy of God, as displayed in the dispensations of His providence and grace, was indeed—more especially in the later years of his life,—the reigning theme of his converse. While, of the counsels of Jehovah at large, embodied in the lively oracles, he could say with truth, "*How precious also are thy thoughts unto me, O God! How great is the sum of them!* the hundred and third Psalm contains the liturgy, to every syllable of which his heart responded with especial emphasis. It were well if in this respect we were all like-minded. Praise is comely for the upright, being—as a spiritual Commentator expresses it—"the only return he can make for his creation, redemption, and all other mercies; the offspring of gratitude, and the expression of love; the elevation of the soul, and the antepast of heaven; its own reward in this life, and an introduction to the felicities of the next." Is there not too much reason to apprehend, my brethren, that criminal deficiency in regard to a duty, recommended and enforced by so many considerations, and so consonant, withal, to the impulses of the regenerate heart in its happiest moments, is among the most prevalent and unsuspected of those *secret faults* from which we must seek to be cleansed, if we would be made perfect in love? He who does not often summon his soul, and all that is within him, to the adoring contemplation and praise of God's wondrous love, as exemplified in the UNSPEAKABLE GIFT, and in the manifold benefits constantly flowing therefrom, will endeavour in vain to rejoice ever more and pray without ceasing.

In an attempt, however brief and incomplete, to appreciate the excellences that commend the example of Mr. Croscombe to our sedulous imitation, those who knew him best will anticipate, at least, a passing reference to his *love for the brethren*—an estimable quality by which he was conspicuously distinguished. Brotherly kindness,—that is to say, the family affection of those who are the children of God by faith in Christ Jesus, is characteristic of all who have passed from death unto life. It is an inseparable concomitant of the love of Him, of whom the whole family in heaven and earth is named; since *filial* love to God involves *fraternal* love to all who exhibit evidence of having received the adoption of sons. This is a principle, superior alike in the spirituality of its nature and the catholicity of its expansion, to all *ecclesiastical* predilections and distinctions. As it has opportunity, it manifests a noble, impartial amity toward *all saints*. Piety, not polity, is the passport to its prompt and loving recognition. Such was one of the dominant elements in the character of the Brother, who, being dead, yet speaketh, by the cherished memory of his benignant brotherly bearing, to all with whom he happened to come in contact who loved our Lord Jesus Christ in sincerity.

I may not, in this connection, pass over in silence his especial affectionate interest in young Ministers, for whom, as knowing their responsibilities and dangers, he always evinced the deepest solicitude. Not a few, now in the palmy days of their sacred career, would, I am quite sure, gladly bear their cordial, consentaneous testimony, to the fidelity and love with which he counselled and encouraged them, at a period when the maxims of experience were, to them, more precious than rubies, and words of comfort, fragrant and soothing as an excellent oil.

With a comprehension of spiritual sympathy that embraced the entire commonwealth of vital Christianity, our now glorified friend associated an ardent admiration and decided preference of the distinctive doctrines, economy and institutions of the

Church of which he was so long a faithful member and an honored minister. Regarding the Founder of our denomination as an anointed and illustrious agent of Divine Providence for inaugurating a new and glorious era in the history of Redemption; and convinced that METHODISM is a restoration in power of Apostolic Christianity; he yielded to no one in attachment whether to its spiritual fellowship, its peculiar principles, or its plans of operation. Its *connexional* bond of unity—its class-meetings, and Love-feasts—its clear annunciation and convincing defence of the faith once delivered to the saints—its offer of a free, full, present, and conscious salvation, to every soul of man;—the godlike catholicity of its genius, and the noble aspirations and achievements of its Missionary spirit,—were so many ligaments that bound his heart to its altars, and made him estimate, next to the privilege of his spiritual relation to God, that of his church relation to Wesleyan Methodism.—And, to the blessed cause, for which he counted not his life dear to himself, he had the happiness and honor of rendering important service in various portions of the globe. In England, his native country; on the Rock of Gibraltar; in Newfoundland; under the subduing summer sun, and amid the winter rigors of the clime of Eastern Canada, as well as in the Provinces of New Brunswick and Nova Scotia; he made full proof of his Ministry: reaping in every place the richest rewards of hallowed toil, in souls saved from death, and churches edified on their most holy faith, by the Divine blessing on his pastoral fidelity.

By the assiduous cultivation of his talents, which were of a respectable order, he overcame to a great extent the disadvantages of an inadequate intellectual preparation for the sacred office; and sustained, with usefulness and honor, a *status* in the Ministry, in advance of many of superior literary attainments. Richly experimental, and faithfully practical, as a *preacher*,—he was worthy of double honor, as, at the same time, a vigilant and affectionate *pastor;* while the purity and elevation of the motive that fed the undying fire of his zeal, were patent to all,—commending him to every man's conscience in the sight of God.

But, on a review, from the bed of death, of his abundant labors, and their gracious results, did he glory in them, think you, as though the *excellency of the power* by which they had been achieved were of himself? The very opposite. Profoundly humbled under a sense of his unworthiness;—feeling that whatever good he had been instrumental in accomplishing, was attributable, not to him, but to the grace of God that was with him;—and full of unfeigned contrition because he had not been more faithful and efficient in the work of the Lord, he died, clinging to the Cross, and glorying only in its redeeming efficacy.

I have done. Accept, beloved friends, as an appropriate application of the solemn subject to which you have given such patient attention, the apostolic monition which, in conclusion, I simply repeat: "Remember them who had the rule over you, who have spoken unto you the word of God, whose faith follow, considering the end of their conversation: Jesus Christ, the same yesterday, and to-day, and forever."